TRANS FORMERS

BUMBLEBEE

Win if You Dare

ORIGINAL GRAPHIC NOVEL

TRANS FORMERS

BUMBLEBEE

Win if You Dare

IDW

Become our fan on Facebook **facebook.com/idwpublishing**
Follow us on Twitter **@idwpublishing**
Subscribe to us on YouTube **youtube.com/idwpublishing**
See what's new on Tumblr **tumblr.idwpublishing.com**
Check us out on Instagram **instagram.com/idwpublishing**

Cover Art by Nicoletta Baldari

Edits by David Mariotte,
Justin Eisinger,
and Alonzo Simon

Design by Tom B. Long

Publisher:
Greg Goldstein

ISBN: 978-1-68405-227-1   21 20 19 18   1 2 3 4

Special thanks to Ben Montano, Josh Feldman, Ed Lane, Beth Artale,
and Michael Kelly for their invaluable assistance

TRANSFORMERS: BUMBLEBEE – WIN IF YOU DARE. SEPTEMBER
2018. FIRST PRINTING. TRANSFORMERS and all related characters
are trademarks of Hasbro and are used with permission. © 2018
Hasbro. All Rights Reserved. Licensed by Hasbro. Trademarks,
design patents and copyrights are used with the approval of the
owner, Volkswagen AG. The IDW logo is registered in the U.S.
Patent and Trademark Office. IDW Publishing, a division of Idea
and Design Works, LLC. Editorial offices: 2765 Truxtun Road, San
Diego, CA 92106. Any similarities to persons living or dead are
purely coincidental. With the exception of artwork used for review
purposes, none of the contents of this publication may be reprinted
without the permission of Idea and Design Works, LLC.
Printed in Canada.
IDW Publishing does not read or accept unsolicited submissions
of ideas, stories, or artwork.

Greg Goldstein, President & Publisher
John Barber, Editor-in-Chief
Robbie Robbins, EVP & Sr. Art Director
Cara Morrison, Chief Financial Officer
Matthew Ruzicka, Chief Accounting Officer
Anita Frazier, SVP of Sales and Marketing
David Hedgecock, Associate Publisher
Jerry Bennington, VP of New Product Development
Lorelei Bunjes, VP of Digital Services
Justin Eisinger, Editorial Director, Graphic Novels & Collections
Eric Moss, Sr. Director, Licensing & Business Development

Ted Adams, Founder & CEO of IDW Media Holdings

For international rights, please contact
licensing@idwpublishing.com

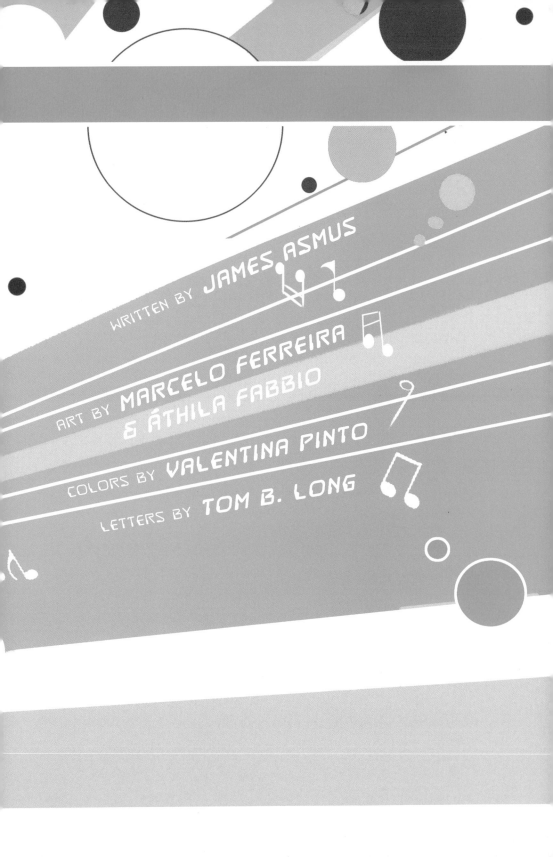

WRITTEN BY JAMES ASMUS

ART BY MARCELO FERREIRA
& ÁTHILA FABBIO

COLORS BY VALENTINA PINTO

LETTERS BY TOM B. LONG

I BELIEVE EVERYONE GETS THEIR *MOMENT*.

A TIME FOR *YOU* TO SHINE.

TO SHOW WHAT YOU'RE MADE OF.

AND IT HAS NOTHING TO DO WITH BEING *"THE BEST."*

IT'S LIKE MUSIC!

SURE, SOME SONGS ARE BETTER THAN OTHERS.

BUT EVEN A TUNE THAT WAS NEVER #1 CAN SOMETIMES BE THE EXACT RIGHT FIT FOR THE MOMENT.

YOU CAN WIN IF YOU DARE!

ANY NEW DEVELOPMENTS, PROWL?

ASIDE FROM WHEELJACK'S REQUEST, MISSIONS ARE STEADY, PRIME.

BUT WE DID PICK UP SOME UNUSUAL SEISMIC ACTIVITY ALONG THE COAST THAT *MIGHT* BE SOME DECEPTICON FUNNY BUSINESS.

ALL RIGHT. WELL, IF YOU TWO ARE RESTED FROM YESTERDAY'S ACTION, WE COULD USE YOUR SPECIALTIES TODAY.

HAPPY TO, OPTIMUS.

GOOD. *WINDBLADE*, FLY OUT TO THE COORDINATES AND SURVEY THE COAST FOR ANY SIGN OF THE DECEPTICONS.

SIDESWIPE. WHEELJACK CALLED FOR A COMPONENT FROM HIS LAB TO PATCH THAT *RADIATION LEAK* IN NEVADA.

YOUR *SPEED* CAN MAKE A BIG DIFFERENCE.

AND, BUMBLEBEE... STAY HERE, AND WE'LL *TALK*.

DON'T FORGET TO *RADIO* IN WITH ANY UPDATES.

THANK YOU— AND *ROLL OUT!*

WAIT—*WHAT?* SEND ME OUT! I'M READY FOR SOMETHING!

EH... SORRY, BEE. I'D OFFER FOR YOU TO TAG ALONG WITH ME, BUT IT SOUNDS LIKE I GOTTA *BURN RUBBER.*

YEAH, AND I GOTTA *FLY.*

WHAT IF I DON'T *WANT* TO TALK?

BUT I'LL LET YOU CHOOSE. YOU CAN DO THEM HERE. *OR—*

RATCHET'S ORDERS ARE—UNLESS THERE WAS AN EMERGENCY— FOR YOU TO *ROAD TEST* YOUR REPAIRS FOR A FEW *HUNDRED MILES* BEFORE GOING BACK INTO ACTION.

YOSEMITE NATIONAL PARK. CALIFORNIA.

OKAY, EARTH. I ADMIT IT—

—YOU'VE GOT SOME PRETTY NICE PLACES FOR AN ALIEN ROBOT TO TRY TO CLEAR HIS HEAD CIRCUITS.

NOT THAT IT'S *WORKING*, SO FAR.

I JUST CAN'T STOP THINKING—

—WOULD OPTIMUS HAVE *SIDELINED* ME LIKE THIS IF I WERE *SIDESWIPE?*

IF I WERE THE *FASTEST*—

—OR THE *SMARTEST*, LIKE WHEELJACK—

—OR THE *STRONGEST*, LIKE GRIMLOCK?

IF THEY THOUGHT I WAS THE *BEST* AT SOMETHING, THEY WOULDN'T BE SO QUICK TO LEAVE ME ON THE *SIDELINES*, WOULD THEY?

BUT I'M *NOT*.

SO THEY *DID*...

"—WHILE WE **TEST DRIVE** YOUR **REPAIRS!**"

SERIOUSLY?

WELL, MY FIGHTS USUALLY INVOLVE LISTENING TO **STARSCREAM.**

AND THAT GUY'S VOICE IS A NIGHTMARE.

BUT YOU SPEND YOUR NIGHTS **RACING!** FROM THE LOOKS OF THINGS, YOU'VE GOT TO BE ONE OF THE FEW COOL PEOPLE IN THIS TOWN!

WELL, IT'S NOT EXACTLY SOMETHING MOST FOLKS **KNOW** ABOUT.

A FEW OF US GO OUT TO THE EMPTY ROADS OUTSIDE OF TOWN—WHERE IT'S SAFER TO FLOOR IT. WE'D JUST TEST SPEED AGAINST SPEED ON STRAIGHTAWAYS. FOR **FUN.**

UNTIL THAT CAR YOU SAW IN YOSEMITE SHOWED UP.

STILL NEVER ACTUALLY **SEEN** THE GUY. BUT HE'S **REAL** COMPETITIVE. HIS RIDE'S TOO HEAVY-DUTY TO BE **SUPER** FAST, BUT HE PLAYS **DIRTY** IF HE THINKS HE MIGHT LOSE.

I BEAT HIM ON A STRAIGHT-AWAY LAST NIGHT. THEN... I THINK HE **FOLLOWED** ME OUT TO THE MOUNTAINS.

I JUST CRUISE THERE TO **RELAX,** BUT...

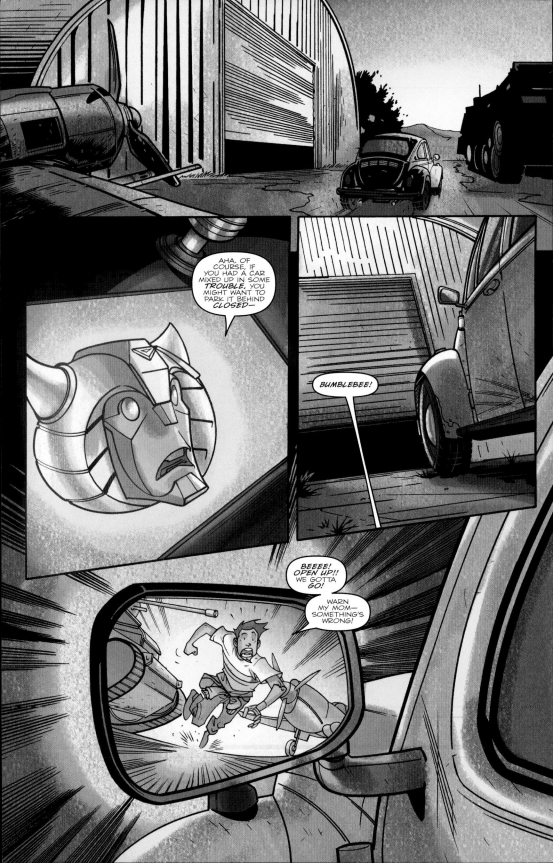

TRY ME.

SHOULD WARN YOU, THOUGH, KID—

—I PREFER DEMOLITION DERBY!

HEY! THAT'S *MY WHEEL* YOU'RE YANKING!

YEAH! TO CATCH HIM ON *MY SHORTCUT!*

BEE? HELP. I... I CAN'T DO IT. I CAN'T *DANCE.*

CAN YOU, LIKE... SET OFF THE FIRE *ALARM,* OR—?

NO WAY, KID! THIS IS WHY WE'RE HERE!

AND *GOOD NEWS*—I MAY NOT BE A TOTAL TECH WHIZ, BUT MY BUDDY WHEELJACK TAUGHT ME ENOUGH...

...THAT I ADDED A *LITTLE* SOMETHING ELSE TO OUR TWO-WAY SIGNALS.

WHAT?!

OH, NO...

OH, *YES.* YOU HIJACKED *MY* STEERING WHEN WE WENT AFTER SWINDLE.

NOW LET *ME* DRIVE.

WHY'S THERE NEVER A DECEPTICON ATTACK WHEN YOU *NEED* ONE?

COME ON! THIS WOULD LOOK *WAY COOLER* IF YOU WORK *WITH* ME.

YOU DIDN'T IN THE *RACE.* I KNOW MY WAY AROUND TOWN!

YOU'RE RIGHT. I SHOULDN'T TRY TO *SHOW OFF.* AT LEAST NOT WHEN—

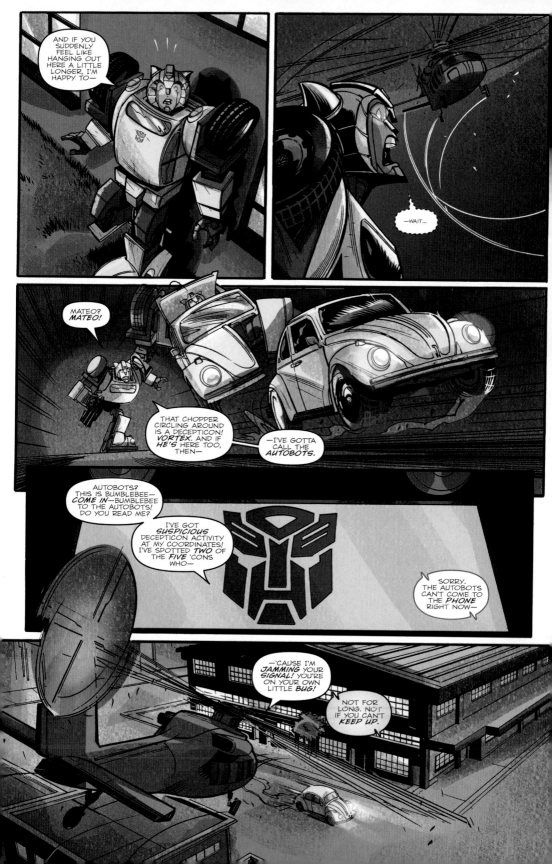

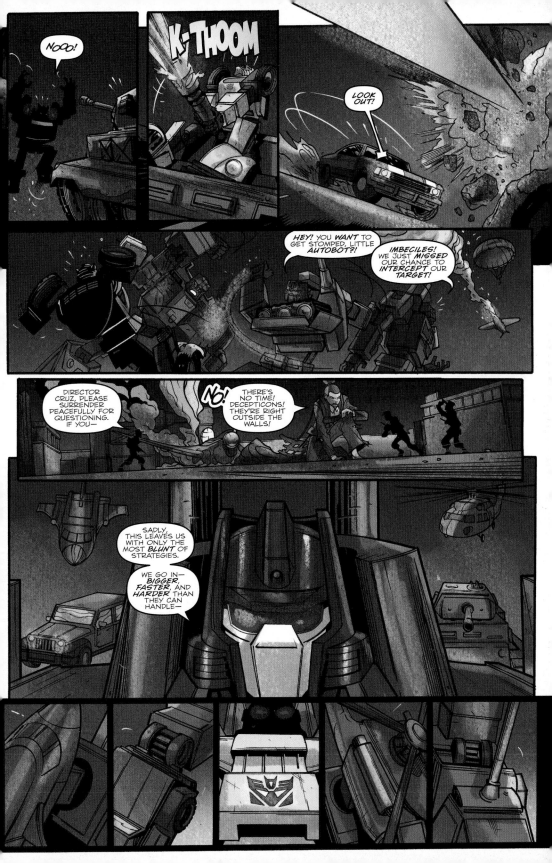

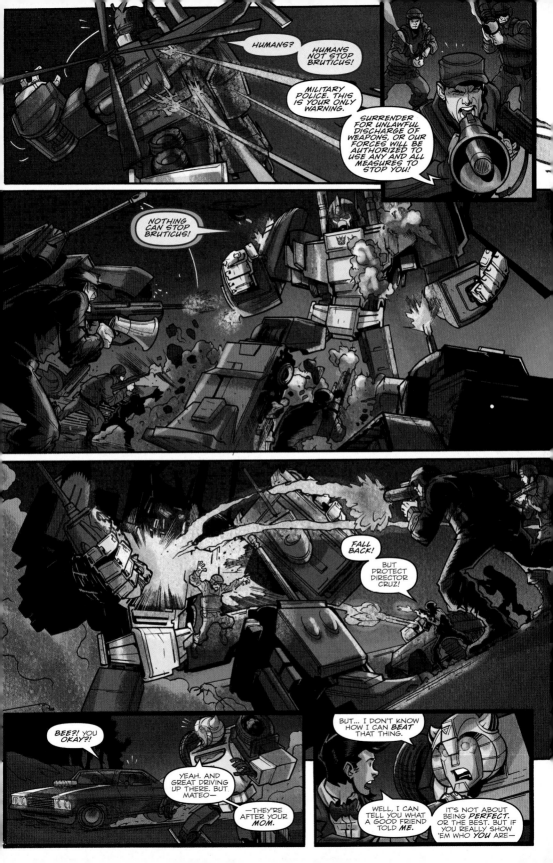

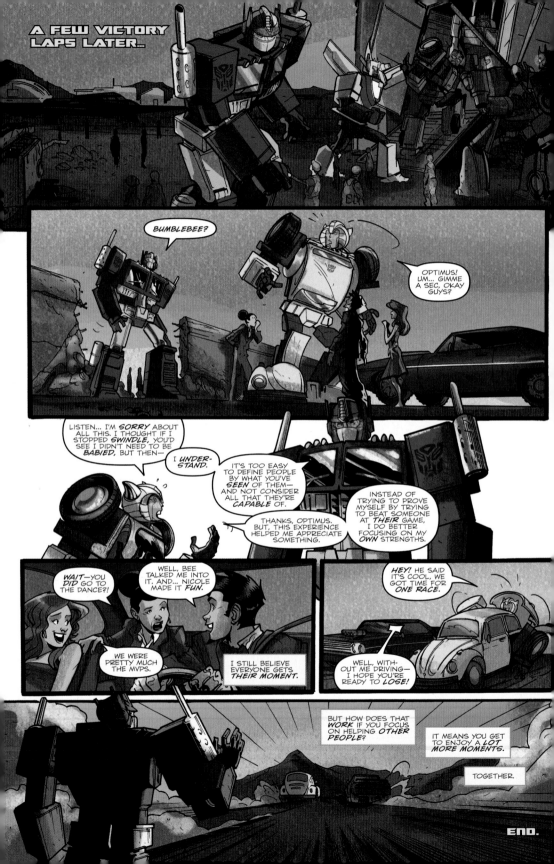

A FEW VICTORY LAPS LATER...

BUMBLEBEE?

OPTIMUS! UM... GIMME A SEC, OKAY GUYS?

LISTEN... I'M *SORRY* ABOUT ALL THIS. I THOUGHT IF I STOPPED *SWINDLE*, YOU'D SEE I DIDN'T NEED TO BE *BABIED*, BUT THEN—

I *UNDER-STAND*.

IT'S TOO EASY TO DEFINE PEOPLE BY WHAT YOU'VE *SEEN* OF THEM— AND NOT CONSIDER ALL THAT THEY'RE *CAPABLE* OF.

INSTEAD OF TRYING TO PROVE MYSELF BY TRYING TO BEAT SOMEONE AT *THEIR* GAME, I DO BETTER FOCUSING ON MY *OWN* STRENGTHS.

THANKS, OPTIMUS. BUT, THIS EXPERIENCE HELPED ME APPRECIATE SOMETHING.

WAIT—YOU *DID* GO TO THE DANCE?!

WELL, BEE TALKED ME INTO IT. AND... NICOLE MADE IT *FUN*.

WE WERE PRETTY MUCH THE MVPS.

I STILL BELIEVE EVERYONE GETS *THEIR MOMENT*.

HEY! HE SAID IT'S COOL, WE GOT TIME FOR *ONE RACE*.

WELL, WITH-OUT ME DRIVING— I HOPE YOU'RE READY TO *LOSE*!

BUT HOW DOES THAT *WORK* IF YOU FOCUS ON HELPING *OTHER PEOPLE*?

IT MEANS YOU GET TO ENJOY *A LOT MORE MOMENTS*.

TOGETHER.

END.

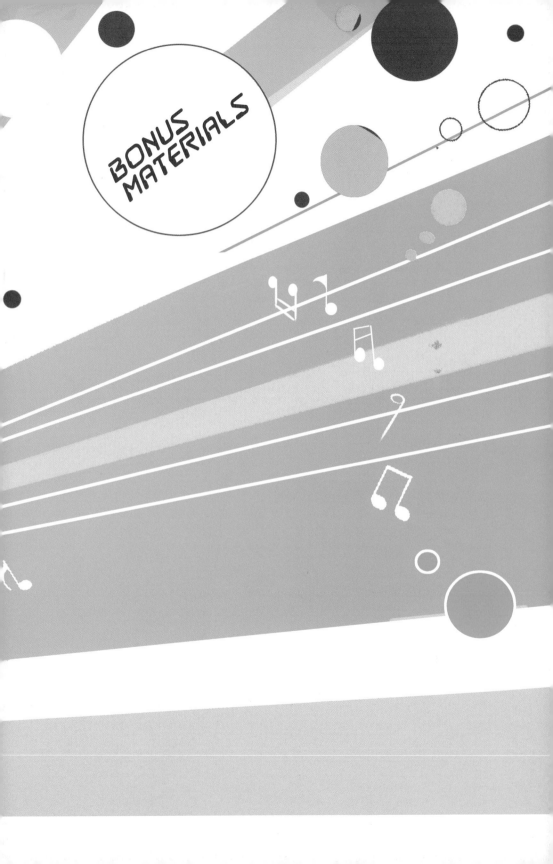

THE PROCESS

Ever wonder how comics are made? Well, as Bumblebee just learned, things work easier with a little bit of teamwork! Now go behind the scenes to see how this team created the story!

The first step of any good comic is figuring out what the story will be and how it'll look! James Asmus, the writer, starts by writing a pitch, just a couple of paragraphs laying out the story as he sees it. Meanwhile, artist Marcelo Ferreira designs Bumblebee's awesome look, establishing the visual mood of the comic!

Then, once the pitch and designs are approved, it's time to get to work on the full story. James Asmus writes the script, laying out the action of each page and the dialogue of the characters. At the left is a page of the script describing when Bumblebee teaches Mateo some sweet dance moves, that then goes to artist Marcelo Ferreira!

PAGE FORTY-FOUR

.1 Okay: here's the pay-off to the high-tech prosthetic plot parallel path – Mateo is frozen, self-conscious on the dance floor, as Nicole just closes her eyes and boogies down next to him. (No one is staring at Mateo – again, kids are wrapped up in their own dramas.) So Mateo is instead pretending to scratch his head to sneak a radio call again.

1. MATEO (small)   Bee? Help. I... I can't do it. I can't <u>dance</u>.

2. MATEO (small)   Can you, like... set off the <u>fire alarm</u>, or—?

2 Outside, Bee looks *excited* as he stands up behind the gym wall, hands out, gearing up to get down!...

3. BEE   <u>No way</u>, kid! <u>This</u> is why we're here!

4. BEE   And <u>good news</u>—I may not be total tech whiz, but my buddy Wheeljack taught me enough...

5. BEE signals.   ...that I added a <u>little</u> something else to our two-way

6. RADIO   <u>What</u>?!

.3 Back inside the dance – Mateo's face is shocked and nervous as he realizes – HIS PROSTHETIC ARM & LEG JUST JUTTED OUT TO HIT the <u>SATURDAY NIGHT FEVER</u> DANCE POSE.

7. MATEO (small)   Oh, no...

4 Outside, Bee grabs one leg (on the same side as Mateo's prosthetics) to do <u>that</u> move—

8. BEE   Oh, <u>yes</u>. You hijacked <u>my</u> steering when we went after Swindle.

9. BEE   Now let <u>me</u> drive.

5 – ??? – Let's do a triptych (maybe borderless?) of Mateo doing different moves, dancing under Bee's lead. Tight shots so that we deliberately don't see the people around him, really (maybe some edges of folks behind him – but not their faces). **Arc these from awkward half-dancing to Mateo decently moving his other limbs to make it all look deliberate.** All the while, though, Mateo whispers through gritted teeth of a scared forced smile to argue with Bee –

10. MATEO (small)   Why's there never a Decepticon attack when you NEED one?

11. BEE (radio/small)   Come on! This would look <u>way cooler</u> if you work <u>with</u> me.

12. MATEO (small)   <u>You</u> didn't in the <u>race</u>. *I* know my way around town!

Marcelo Ferreira's role as the line-artist is a multi-step process. First, he begins by doing a rough layout of the pages as they'll appear. The first stages, called thumbnails, can be very loose sketches, just laying out the basic design of the page. Here we have a bunch of happy silhouettes doing some quick moves!

Once the thumbs are approved, Marcelo goes on to pencils—solidifying the figures and designs from his sketches—and then to inks, where characters and background take on real depth, becoming the fully formed figures you see on the page! And then it's on to the next step, Valentina Pinto adds color!

Though Valentina Pinto doesn't step in until after the inks are done, she's an equally important part of the comics making process! As good as the inks look, they just wouldn't be as fun without colors!

From the early stages, Valentina works on giving a unique look to the pages—here using a textured, chalky coloring palette to make the book fun and bright in a way that looks different from other comics! Among her other jobs, she also makes decisions based on lighting—see how the colors change as Mateo moves under the disco ball!

Finally, once all the art is done, the book enters production. Letterer and designer Tom B. Long not only puts all the dialogue James Asmus wrote onto the art from Marcelo Ferreira and Valentina Pinto, but also assembles every part of the book!

From the lettering, the whole creative team, the editor, and the team at Hasbro all take another look—checking for typos and other errors. If everything looks right and there are no changes, the book is officially complete!

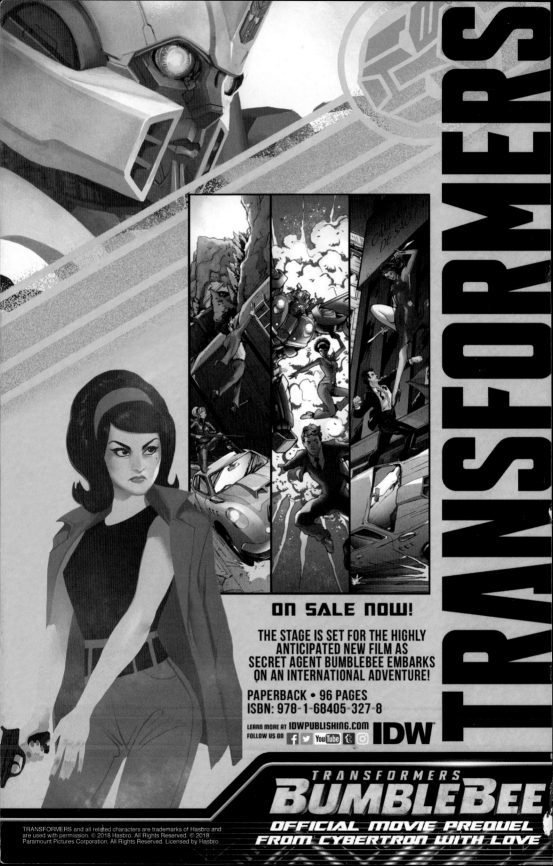